CHRISTMAS 2015
You are 4½ years old!

The Fairy Princess

Sparkles in the Snow

by Julie Andrews & Emma Walton Hamilton

Illustrated by
Christine Davenier

Little, Brown and Company
New York Boston

Hi! I'm Geraldine, and I'm a fairy princess.
It's just a feeling that I have inside, something
SPARKLY that's hard to explain.

Like all fairy princesses, I spend a lot of time
caring for my subjects and making them feel happy.
(Fairy princesses try to spread joy and wonder
whenever and wherever they can!)

SPEAKING of wonder, we're having a Winter Wonderland Festival at our school! There will be ice sculptures, arts and crafts, a bake sale, and sleigh rides.

Best of all, there's going to be a concert—
and I get to sing with the chorus!
(Fairy princesses are at their SPARKLIEST
when expressing themselves in song.)

I just KNOW that Mr. Higginbottom, our music teacher,
is going to choose ME to sing the solo.
He always says I am the most ENTHUSIASTIC singer in our school!
So far, he hasn't announced his choice, so I'm trying to make his job easier.
(Fairy princesses know how hard it is to remember all the details.)

During rehearsal, I step out just a bit and
sing in my BEST voice.
Mr. Higginbottom reminds me that many
voices in a chorus need to sound like ONE.

At lunchtime, I stroll past his office door.
I sing a happy tune while pretending to tie my shoe.
He waves, but keeps working at his desk.

At recess, I stand underneath his window and sing my LOUDEST.
I guess the playground is so noisy that he doesn't hear me.

The next day, Mr. Higginbottom tells us that a PROFESSIONAL singer is coming from the city to be our guest soloist.

He says she will be a "big draw" for the concert.
I think it sounds like a big DRAG.
(Even a fairy princess can forget her manners
when she's disappointed.)

Mommy tells me not to be sad. The whole family will be coming, and their eyes will be on ME.
Daddy says I'll always be HIS star.
My brother, Stewart, says at least now I won't get bigheaded.
This does not make me feel better.

On the morning of the concert, I wake up to a surprise.
It's SNOWING!
Just what a Winter Wonderland needs!
Maybe it won't be such a bad day after all.
(Fairy princesses know how to take a frown and turn it upside down.)

Daddy and Stewart shovel the driveway and warm up the car.
Mommy packs up the goodies she made for the bake sale.
I put on my velvet dress and big, furry snow boots.
Then I do my vocal warm-ups.
(A fairy princess is always well prepared!)

It takes TWICE as long as usual to get to school because of the snow.
When we enter the Great Hall, I hardly recognize it!
There are fairy lights on all the booths, and shimmering ice sculptures
that look like statues from a royal palace.

Everything smells like cinnamon, gingerbread, and chocolate.
I have to admit, it does look pretty WONDER-ful.

But Mr. Higginbottom looks worried.
He tells us our guest soloist is stuck in the snow
and won't make it on time.
I offer to sing in her place if that would help.
(Fairy princesses are ALWAYS happy to lend a hand in a crisis.)

He nods at me and says to put our belongings in the locker room and be on stage in five minutes. I think I might EXPLODE with sparkle!

I take off my coat and snow boots, and open my backpack.
But…where are my dress-up shoes?
Oh NO! I must have left them at home!
What a DISASTER!

I can't go on stage in my big, furry snow boots!
Even worse, my socks don't match, and there's a hole in the big toe!
This is going to be the most UN-wonderful day EVER!
But…there must be SOMETHING I can do.
After all, I AM a fairy princess!

I peek out of the locker room and see the arts and crafts table.
Suddenly I get an idea.
I DASH over to it and grab some purple poster paint and a brush.

I quickly paint a ballet slipper on each sock.
(I have to paint my big toe as well.)
It's not perfect, but it will have to do.
The concert is about to start!

We walk out on stage in a long line.
When it's time for my solo, I take a few steps forward.
Mr. Higginbottom lifts his baton, smiles at me, then raises an eyebrow.
There is a trail of purple footprints all across the stage!
Some of the other singers giggle.
I feel my sparkle beginning to disappear.

My face feels hot and my ears start burning.
But the orchestra begins to play…
and the music is SO pretty.

I look up and see all the smiling faces
and all the twinkling lights in front of me.
Suddenly my sparkle comes RUSHING back.
I take a deep breath…and I sing, and I sing, and I SING!

After the concert, Mr. Higginbottom
gives me a big high five!

Daddy says I stole the show, and Mommy hugs me
and helps me into my snow boots.
Stewart says my painted socks were a pretty good idea,
but they didn't fool HIM.

We buy hot chocolate and cinnamon buns. YUM!
Then we bundle into a sleigh.
The snow is still falling, the jingle bells make their own music, and we all sing a sleighing song together.
It doesn't get more winter wonderful than this!

I guess the SPARKLIEST things can happen when you least expect them!

For Patti Ann, who makes a wonderland of all *our books.*

—J.A. & E.W.H.

Pour Mimi à qui je pense si fort en cette période de Noël et qui fait bien sûr partie de mes merveilleux souvenirs d'enfance en Touraine.

—C.D.

About This Book

The illustrations for this book were done in ink and color pencil on Kaecolor paper. The text was set in Baskerville and the display type is Mayfair. As she worked on this book, Christine Davenier thought of her childhood memories of magic and Christmas lights and scents, and had her Maurice Sendak, Richard Scarry, Eva Eriksson, and Gabrielle Vincent books pulled from her shelves and opened next to her table for inspiration.

This book was edited by Liza Baker and designed by Patti Ann Harris. The production was supervised by Jonathan Lopes, and the production editor was Christine Ma.

 • Little, Brown and Company • Hachette Book Group • 237 Park Avenue, New York, NY 10017 • Visit our website at www.lb-kids.com • Little, Brown and Company is a division of Hachette Book Group, Inc. • The Little, Brown name and logo are trademarks of Hachette Book Group, Inc. • The publisher is not responsible for websites (or their content) that are not owned by the publisher. • First Edition: October 2013 • Library of Congress Cataloging-in-Publication Data • Andrews, Julie. • The very fairy princess sparkles in the snow / Julie Andrews & Emma Walton Hamilton ; illustrated by Christine Davenier.—1st ed. • p. cm. • Summary: Gerry, a most enthusiastic singer, is certain her music teacher will choose her to perform the solo at the Winter Wonderland Festival, and when someone else is chosen it takes a snowfall to bring Gerry's sparkle back. • ISBN 978-0-316-21963-1 • [1. Concerts—Fiction. 2. Singing—Fiction. 3. Princesses—Fiction.] I. Hamilton, Emma Walton. II. Davenier, Christine, ill. III. Title. • PZ7.A5673Vh 2013 • [E]—dc23 • 2012042576 • 10 9 8 7 6 5 4 3 2 1 • SC • Printed in China